The Bhogmon Eat Book!

Chinmay Chakravarty

Ukiyoto Publishing

All global publishing rights are held by

Ukiyoto Publishing

Published in 2023

Content Copyright © Chinmay Chakravarty

ISBN 9789360160814

All rights reserved.
No part of this publication may be reproduced, transmitted, or stored in a retrieval system, in any form by any means, electronic, mechanical, photocopying, recording or otherwise, without the prior permission of the publisher.

The moral rights of the authors have been asserted.

This is a work of fiction. Names, characters, businesses, places, events, locales, and incidents are either the products of the author's imagination or used in a fictitious manner. Any resemblance to actual persons, living or dead, or actual events is purely coincidental.

This book is sold subject to the condition that it shall not by way of trade or otherwise, be lent, resold, hired out or otherwise circulated, without the publisher's prior consent, in any form of binding or cover other than that in which it is published.

www.ukiyoto.com

To my wife Ragini Bhattacharyya Chakravarty for all the help n servings on all possible fronts--from music to writing and to the delicacies cooked in her kitchen!

Contents

Syndrome Of The Fish Fin!	1
Chickened Out!	7
Essence Of Life Is Rice!	17
About the Author	26

Syndrome of the Fish Fin!

Bhogmon has been getting used to lunching at various restaurants near his office neighborhood of the big city, somewhere in Assam; because he hates carrying the *dabba* or the tiffin box every day all the way to office from home. It's not that his doting mother doesn't make him his favorite dishes; she does and is ready to do it every day of his working week but for his unwillingness to carry. He also wholeheartedly hates the practice of eating lunch with his office mates for the simple reason that they keep on snatching at each other's tiffin boxes for what they proclaim 'only to taste how your wife/mother cooks' and during that unfortunate process he very often misses taking even a single substantial bite of the delicious dish his mother prepares for his exclusive benefit and has to remain contented with the random deliverance of the varied bits from his mates' boxes that he mostly dislikes. Besides, there's another more worrying angle to the box he carries: irrespective of how watertight he seals it and irrespective of how deep the steel container lies inside his backpack the familiar vapid smell never stops confronting his nosy apparatus and most probably spreading to other noses around whenever he happens to open his bag inside the crowded bus confines or in the jam-packed train compartments.

Then of course, as the true connoisseur of good food that he always compliments himself with he loves variety. Not that he gets tired of his mother's cooking, but apart from the carrying hassles he doesn't at all mind the differential richness of the tastes he gets at the restaurants.

That day was not different. Feeling the healthy pangs of hunger even before the lunch hour, Bhogmon gets out of the office alone; yes, he always discourages anyone willing to give him company, and he takes great delight in the general tendency of the office people to avoid spending the unnecessary bucks eating out. The other day when he was just out of a lunch joint, he met a college friend and during their casual conversation the friend told him that he should definitely try a very good and homely hotel which is a little farther down the road.

So, today Bhogmon entered that hotel and was immediately fascinated by the welcoming aroma lingering in the cozy interior. Greatly inspired by the smells galore and his prompting taste buds he ordered fish curry as the main dish along with the rice plate. As is customary with such food joints the general rice plate comes first and the main dish follows moments later.

Bhogmon, the hungry pangs intensifying inside him, got busy immediately as the rice plate was placed on the table first. He very much liked the homely pulses curry and the vegetable items, and as he relished licking his fingers the main fish curry bowl arrived by his side. Filled with an overwhelming feeling of trust in the new aromatic place he didn't even bother to take a look, and decided to finish his eating foreplay first.

Bhogmon liked the look of the fish curry instantly: the thick yellowish-brownish gravy filling the ceramic bowl and the fish piece submerged in it in all its appetizing tenderness. He spread the remaining mound of rice across his plate and then took the bowl, pouring the contents over in true gourmet anticipation. However, as the hidden piece touched down on his rice-land and became immensely visible to his devouring eyes, he reacted as if a sudden attack of paralysis took complete control of his body.

Hey! What the heck! He exclaimed in silent agony. He wanted to call the waiters and shout it out to them; but as the paralysis eased a bit, he discovered better common sense in not creating a scene that could be more embarrassing for him than for the other eaters. He made up his mind to announce this anomaly loud and clear while settling the bill with the counter manager later. He resumed his eating, even though he still looked angrily at the fish fin piece lying innocently on his plate.

He remembers what his mother usually did to such pieces of the fish: she always reserved that piece for herself, because she could never offer it to the head of the household as he'd find it messy and time-consuming, and neither to her children as it was risky for them. The tail piece is always full of fishbone and thorns or *kaantas* and it was also considered inauspicious for the guests. He remembers all the politics involved in what he merrily calls the piece-distribution strategy that entailed the best meaty pieces go to the head householder followed in close proximity by the children—first boys and then girls if any—and the important guests in the rather uncanny order of ladies second. The scenario gets all the more complicated with the arrivals of daughters-in-law and grandchildren if the inhabitants still stick to the joint family norms, Bhogmon being a living witness of the process happening in his own household. The piece-distribution strategy gets transferred inexorably to that of the eldest daughters-in-law changing the priorities thereby in favor of their sons and husbands, followed by the former head householders and then finally the ladies in the traditional order as mentioned above. The fish head was not a problem, because his mother like possibly all mothers and wives used to make a deliciously thick spicy curry of the boiled and then mashed fish head. He also remembers the even more complicated politics involving the distribution of chicken pieces in domestic circles which would also make an exciting story. Fortunately, we've decided to include that story too here as a tribute to our eat-hero Bhogmon.

Now! A supposedly reputed hotel is dishing out that unwelcome piece to him! How come! How is it possible at all? He couldn't believe such a thing had happened to him, although he continued eating in the healthiest of manners.

The time of the unavoidable confrontation arrived as he finished his meal, washed hands and mouth and drying those approached the manager.

"So, you treat your esteemed guests with thorny fish tail pieces here?" he addressed him in the most menacing way he thought he was capable of, although keeping his voice low.

"Any problem, Sir?" the manager asked politely.

Bhogmon dug into his purse to find an appropriate currency note while continuing the unpleasant conversation, "You see! Even in our home we don't serve the tail pieces of a fish to our non-paying guests! And your boys never care a damn serving those to your heavily-paying customers!" he continued after reluctantly handing over the note, "How can you do that?"

The manager deposited the note into the cash drawer under the counter desk and replied in a philosophical way, "You see, sir! The tail or the fin is also an integral part of the fish!"

That remark made Bhogmon furious. He nearly blurted out, "Then why the hell didn't you serve me the full goddamn fish head on a platter instead?" He checked himself in time, because he knew very well that heads of big fishes are not served as standalones, and instead are made into a curry called *ghanta*. Therefore, he made himself make an alternative expression of his fury.

"Okay, if you take that line of approach then I must say I am also a part of your clientele…rather I was!" he took the change, "Means I'll never come here again and will also advise my friends not to!"

"Sir! You should've checked the piece when the boy brought it to your table."

Bhogmon conceded that. He paused momentarily at the exit and quipped looking back at the manager. "I thought I could trust you!"

Chickened Out!

The sparkling red Hyundai Creta stopped near the main market of the city. It was around 8 in the evening. Bhogmon's brother-in-law, a tall dark-complexioned man of athletic build and around 45 years of age, parked the SUV nicely in a vacant spot and got out telling him it'd take only a few minutes. His eldest brother-in-law, Aniket, kept the engine going so that Bhogmon could wait in air-conditioned comfort. Bhogmon didn't know about this scheduled or unscheduled stop as he watched Aniket head toward a restaurant. Maybe his eldest sister Rekha asked her husband to bring in some food items for their two boys, he thought.

Bhogmon decided to visit her sister that weekend as his mother had gone to their native village home where his eldest brother managed the household as well as what remained of the farming activities. His father was a very successful farmer and wanted his three sons to maintain his multi-crop cultivation farm. However, his dream was only partially realized: his middle son got a good officer's job in the state government and had to leave the village; the youngest offspring Bhogmon landed a job in a private firm and had to rent a house in the big city; and only the eldest son, unable to complete his studies, remained in the village, got married and settled there. Several plots of paddy fields had to be sold off in due course of time to provide for the medical expenses of their ailing father and to marry off the three daughters. Barely into his sixties their father died a frustrated man a few years back and since then his mother had been passing her time or more appropriately, spending her life, staying with her three sons on a non-specific rotation, and occasionally visiting a random daughter.

Earlier in the evening Rekha ordered him to pay a visit to their ever-complaining maternal aunt and arranged with Aniket to take him there. His aunt, younger to his mother, was very happy to see him and treated them to a sumptuous snack of *luchi-bhaji* and an assortment of homemade *laddus* along with steaming cups of tea. It'd been about two hours since that meal was taken and Bhogmon was already looking forward to a delicious dinner as he waited in the car.

After around fifteen minutes that Bhogmon didn't mind waiting out Aniket came back with a big shining silver foil packet and put the parcel tenderly opposite the gear box. He mumbled some sort of an informal apology to Bhogmon for the wait and moved the car briskly away.

Bhogmon's sensitive nosy apparatus was very able to catch the mildest of fragrances emanating from the sealed packet, and he instantly interpreted it as a most welcome one: the aroma of a flaming hot ready-to-eat Tandoori Chicken. His taste buds got into an overdrive immediately and began producing the hunger pangs—a bit prematurely though, considering the still unabsorbed food particles in his stomach. But in the spirit of a true connoisseur of all good food he was already preparing himself for a roaring starter at the supper tonight. Those 15 minutes that Aniket took to reach home proved to be much more longer for Bhogmon than on the earlier occasion.

They all lounged in the living room sofa after refreshing and changing clothes with Bhogmon waiting for the dinner to be served sooner than later, because he was worried the beauty of the starter item would increasingly lose its value as the minutes ticked by. The silver parcel disappeared somewhere in the kitchen after Aniket handed it over to his wife. Perhaps, Rekha was going to keep it warm inside some OTG or microwave, he thought hopefully.

More than an hour passed. There was still no sign of any positive dinning-table activities. Rekha was carrying on with her normal kitchen chores—the sounds of frying something, the whistles of a pressure cooker and the clanking of utensils only coming out from her arena.

Bhogmon was getting more and more uneasy all the time while Aniket lay on the sofa, absolutely unperturbed and expressionless, fiddling with his smartphone. He desperately needed to remind Rekha of the impending danger that could cause a permanent damage to the intrinsic delights of the starter; but he refrained from interfering as had been his wont with all independent households, irrespective of to whom those belonged.

And definitely no games with Rekha, he warned himself against any possible slip of words. Yes! Rekha! He mused: she'd been the most discontented and the ever-complaining child of their family; she always wanted all the comforts that could be made available, even if that couldn't be afforded; his father bought the first ever table fan of the house—just for the comfort of Rekha, whereas there'd still been not a single ceiling fan in the house; she always extricated a bit more in everything managed by their parents for all the members of the household, say in terms of an additional item in the meals or a better-quality dress on festive occasions or a more comfortable pair of chappals or some pricey cosmetic items; and, Bhogmon remembers clearly even now, her eternal vow, always expressed loud and frequently, that she'd make dead sure to give her own children all the things aplenty that she was deprived of in her childhood or even older days.

After nine-thirty in the evening the dining table finally witnessed some activity. More than two hours now that the lovely dish had been made to lie low. However, things that happened minutes later horrified Bhogmon, instead of the culinary delights he anticipated.

The dinner turned out to be as normal as it used to be in most days—the omnipresent dal-rice, one or two vegetable items and the fish curry. There was no indication of a starter. This time Bhogmon could no longer stick on to his policy of non-interference.

"Hey *baideo*! What has happened to the Tandoori item that *bhindeo* brought, I suppose?" he asked, trying to keep his voice low and as much in a casual tone as possible.

Rekha didn't look up at him, but only shouted out, "Boys! Do you want your bites now? ... okay! come down and take your plates!" she rose and went to the kitchen. She returned with the silver foil parcel along with two flowered ceramic dishes. She opened the packet and started arranging the pieces in the two plates. The younger boy descended from their room upstairs and joined her mother giving me a sweet smile. "Wait!" Rekha delved into the packet and finding a splinter piece put that on my plate. Then to her husband she said, "You'd too like to have a piece?" Aniket shook his head, and Bhogmon, watching the proceedings in fascination, was not sure if that shake of his head was formed out of habit or out of accumulated frustration and anger.

Rekha finally said, "Okay! Take the plates and the packet! Have your fill, but don't overeat, right? You can eat the rest in the morning!"

Bhogmon engaged himself eating silently as all the attributes of his wonderful sister came flooding back into his mind. Yes! So true to her noble vow—never ever deprive the dear sons of anything in life! However, that thought had brought in its wake another observation that Bhogmon finds really perplexing: that the modern-age kids are obsessively fond of chicken and that, unlike in the childhood days of Bhogmon and his siblings, these modern-day kids decide what food is good for them and dictate their parents to arrange those on a daily basis; they order for chicken in almost every meal and their parents oblige in the most endearing way, like they normally used to collect bones or odd pieces on a daily basis for their pets, and now, thanks to the changing times the pets are rocking as they find normal flesh and bones daily.

Perhaps, Bhogmon's thinktank went on, this digital-age obsession of the children makes the chicken piece-distribution strategy somewhat easier, meaning the prime pieces or almost the whole of it go only to the kids, as if depriving the adults including all the important males were no sin at all! Bhogmon finds no answer to this puzzle: why such obsession? Still in the late twenties Bhogmon too belongs to the modern age more or less, but in his childhood days there were no demands made on their parents to make special dishes for them; they all accepted whatever was decided by their parents—in food, clothes, education and all that. Maybe, with some rare exceptions like Rekha, but now those exceptions are becoming the rule, Bhogmon muses on.

Bhogmon knows about the politics of the chicken-distribution strategy under normal circumstances only too well: the strategy follows the same trajectory like that of the fish-distribution strategy except for the glaring inequality that in case of chicken the available prime pieces are extremely limited—only two, to be precise—as the poor bird can provide only two legs; so, the presence of the various males of importance and their offspring in a traditional household, plus guests on occasion, makes the distribution dicey and dangerous; and many vexed householders are forced to ask the butchers to chop it up in the smallest of pieces as is humanly possible so that no earthly souls are able to discern which were legs and which were not. But now, Bhogmon concludes happily, the digital-age obsession makes it much easier and wholly less clumsy. Reserve all of the pieces for the kids and dish out the rest to the adults like Rekha did to him with that splinter, he thinks with a silent groan. However, he reminds himself sternly, it's not that he hates the kids; in fact, he loves them and gets along with them in the most friendliest and communicating of ways.

Two factors irritated him to no less measure. If it was to be purchased exclusively for the kids why was he made to undergo the torture inside the car and why not the restaurant asked for home delivery with or without his knowledge? Then, the behavior of his dear sister who he thinks still loves him was amazing: she gave him a splinter piece in a most disdainful manner like throwing the grains at the turkey itself and never bothered to ask him if he needed more or how he liked it!

Bhogmon decided on his course of action and maintained his orchestrated silence as he finished his meal and quickly retired to the bedroom where he stayed whenever he visited his sister. He was very desirous of making his sentimental glumness known and felt by his sister, like in the way in the old days when the kids got sentimental or fell ill they were showered with an avalanche of attention. But, he thought ruefully, that no longer holds nowadays, in spite of the unprecedented focus upon the children by their parents in any sphere of activity—another puzzle of sorts for him. Maybe the utter absence of the smartphones or other gadgets in those days made the sentiments easily accessible to the persons in command, he wondered.

*

It was a Sunday the next day. To his chagrin, Bhogmon had to get up early because Rekha had already scheduled a trip to the nearest hill city—mostly for marketing of woollens with the winter approaching in about two months. However, Bhogmon knew it very well that the actual purpose of the trip was to give a sumptuous treat to the kids in one of the most famous restaurants of the city. And the treat would obviously consist of the rich varieties of chicken, chicken and only chicken, he grimaced.

Bhogmon stuck to his show of unabashed ill-humor—at the breakfast table, at the back of the car with the kids on each side of his, at the unknown joints on the way for tea breaks, during the hectic marketing forays and finally, at the sparkling spacious air-conditioned restaurant.

As anticipated by him, they started ordering starters and main dishes in kind of a spell—all mostly chicken. They were occupying a rectangular table with Rekha and Aniket on one side and Bhogmon along with the two boys facing them. Rekha found herself fully immersed with the errands of the boys while Aniket asked him for his choice. Bhogmon announced a shade louder than usual that he'd take only veg items, just dal-rice. Nobody asked him why so that his last-ditch attempt to show his sentiments failed yet again.

The younger kid loved the Crispy Baby Corn dish and accordingly the doting parents ordered a plate along with many other plates. Since the baby corn dish was a vegetarian dish the waiter moved it around the table distributing to all. Bhogmon noticed that Rekha refused to have any of that, and therefore, when the waiter came to him, he allowed him to give just a few pieces. He was aware that Rekha was alternately staring at him and at his plate.

Rekha was of a short stature and getting all the fatter as her age was increasing. She was at a disadvantage to keep up the vigil on Bhogmon: since she was short her vision was getting obstructed by the jutting water bottles and jars on the table; and she was trying her best to peek through any available gaps in the assembly like the crowds move their heads left and right in a football match to follow the action to have a cognizant view on his eating. Bhogmon understood that she was extremely concerned lest her boys, especially the younger one, got much lesser shares of the baby corns thanks to the public distribution.

Now plainly irritated but not at all in denial of his great love for the crispy corns, Bhogmon poised his fork on a piece as the eyes of Rekha continued playing hide and seek through the bottled wall. Perhaps due to his mounting discontent caused by the indiscreet stares Bhogmon's fork slipped over a crispy-red piece and the ill-fated piece shot off finally settling itself under the table. Cursing himself Bhogmon ensured the remaining pieces go into his mouth safely, come what may. You like it or not, peeping sis! He mocked in deadly silence.

The chicken orgy was in full swing as Bhogmon was halfway through his dal-rice meal. Suddenly, Aniket who had had his share of the chicken pieces this time looked up at Bhogmon saying,

"Hey bro! Why don't you try some of the chicken dishes here? Excellent, I assure you! And what is so hard and fast about your sudden whim for vegetarian dishes, eh?"

Bhogmon forced a smile and took a look at the bowls on the table. All of those were devoid of any chicken pieces or even bones by now! He thought angrily, "Piece of shit! You want me to taste the useless gravy only, the leftovers!" loud, he said, "No *bhindeo*! No use tempting me! I'm committed to a veg meal today, and I'm having that only!" and he thanked no one.

Essence Of Life Is Rice!

That Friday evening Bhogmon left office early to catch the last bus to his native village. His mother had been staying there for some time now. So, he decided to visit his village home during that weekend taking a casual leave on Monday and to bring her back to his flat in the city. He'd been in touch with her over telephone every alternate day and she was always worrying about what he must have been eating all these days. Bhogmon always told her not to worry; but did not tell her the whole truth that in fact he'd been greatly enjoying tasting various types of food in many more new restaurants he'd discovered and there was also the bonus of getting invited to relatives' and friends' places for dinners giving him one more richer window to enjoy more varieties of food. But of course, he does miss his mother's unique cooking, he assures himself.

He always loves to be home, not just for the food which is no doubt pure and its taste pristine. He loves the environs too—the large campus, the olden tin-roofed house with half brick walls and at least a dozen small-big rooms, the flower and fruit garden in front of the house, the fresh-water pond at the backyard, the well in the inner courtyard, the three-compartment kitchen complex and so on. And then the walks in the farming fields the number of which has reduced greatly over the years though.

His eldest brother, Rongmon, in his early fifties, is very hard-working and a jovial man. In fact, he was such a happy baby, always smiling and laughing at the beholders, that their father named him Rongmon. His middle brother, Khagen, in his early forties, was different, and there was a history about his name. He was such an angry baby always scowling at and refusing the beholders point-blank that their father named him Khongmon. When in high school Khongmon started detesting his name so violently that his father was forced to resort to all legal options to change his name to Khagen. And Bhogmon was named like that because he's been always so fond of food, and since his birth his parents never had any problem feeding him with whatever was available. Rongmon's wife Charu is a my-dear lady and a perfect homemaker. They have three kids—two sons and a daughter. The daughter, the eldest, is studying at the town college and the two sons are in the local high school.

They were all waiting for him for supper when he reached home. Normally, they take dinner quite early, say around 8 in the evening as the village still goes to sleep early. Ten o' clock is very late for them; but they, particularly his mother, cannot afford to let the youngest and the dearest son of the family who is coming home after a long break eat alone. And so, all of them had a lovely dinner together.

Bhogmon was so happy to find his mother preparing his favorite curry of a variety of small fish.

Bhogmon planned to spend the two days of his stay there fully indoors, just enjoying the food, the company and the ambience. But his middle brother Khagen rang him up first thing in the morning inviting him for lunch on Sunday. Since the last few months Khagen had been serving in the small township, just 10 miles away from their home, as a revenue officer. Khagen also offered to pick him up with his bike, but Bhogmon asked him not to take the trouble as he'd ride their father's bicycle that they preserved with love and respect for the short journey, bicycle ride being one of his most favorite pastimes whenever he comes home.

Bhogmon didn't have many opportunities to meet his sister-in-law, Khagen's wife Renu, because of their frequent transfers across the state; he met her only at the occasional social functions that mostly did not offer enough time for a personal conversation. But he has heard a lot of good things about her: she's educated with a degree; she has a progressive mindset not hesitating to do jobs like stitching, taking tuitions, going to the markets to buy even groceries, fish and all that; and she is very social, polite and cordial to his mother and to all the in-laws, never giving them any scope for any complaint or murmurs in secret domestic circles in her married life of more than ten years.

*

Khagen, Renu and their 9-year-old daughter Maina came out to greet Bhogmon as he announced his arrival by joyfully ringing the bicycle bell in continuous short spells. They all laughed as they went inside. Bhogmon was about to sit down on the sofa when Renu made a sudden observation, "Well, Mon! mind your belly! It seems to be showing signs of getting fatter!"

Before Bhogmon, a little taken aback, could answer Khagen grinned and said, "You see, Mon! your sis has seriously taken to dieting and fitness! I've also been under her constant observation nowadays! But don't worry! You can take care after getting married!"

The conversation went on in a lively and homely manner with the mandatory tea break in-between. Having the opportunity to be able to spend some good time with his sister-in-law Bhogmon discussed a lot of things with her, and at one point he joked about the name-changer story of Khagen.

"*Bou*! Do you know the original name our father gave to him?"

"Yes, of course! He actually did a wrong thing by refusing a paternal name! what's in a name, you tell me?" Renu teased.

"So, you'd have loved him still if he had come to you as Khongmon?" Bhogmon threw it back even as Khagen scowled at him.

"Why not? As I said what's in a name!"

"But I hope *majuda* doesn't still have his bouts of hot temper?"

"Much under control nowadays! Particularly after I advised him to show that temper to his bosses and the visiting ministers!"

All of them laughed. Shortly afterward Renu went to the kitchen for the final preparations, and minutes later invited them all to the dining table. Maina came forward to help her mother set the table. As Bhogmon washed his hands and sat at the allotted chair he was happy to see the plates, the pots and the white ceramic bowls set elegantly and invitingly on the table. He took a note of the things on offer as he's been used to: apart from the dal-rice there are two preparations of brinjal fries and cauliflower-potato *bhaji*; there was a bowl containing the fish curry and another of most probably mutton; there was a large plate containing beetroot-cucumber-tomato-carrot salad with a few pieces of lemon; and the then the bigger rice bowl.

Although his tastes buds were fully activated with rapt anticipation the last detail concerned Bhogmon a bit. Renu was distributing rice from the bowl: the largest portion on his plate, a little lesser on Khagen's, lesser still on Maina's and the tiniest portion on her own plate. The reverse was the order in case of the salad—the large portions to Khagen and Maina and the largest to herself—and leaving Bhogmon help himself for his portion.

It was the situation with the rice bowl that continued to concern him. He expected Renu to take the near-empty bowl to the kitchen for a refill; however, instead of doing that she indifferently put the bowl on the table and took her seat.

Bhogmon's mind raced. He feared the worst. It was probable that the bowl contained the entire rice cooked and there were no grains left or there was still some rice in the cooker and she'd refill at a later stage, depending on the demand situation. Bhogmon is no taker for chances. He took it to himself that there was no more rice for which now he was going to have to initiate some sort of a rationing for his portion of rice, meaning he was going to have to devote the least portion for the dal-indulgence as that item is too common and present almost with every meal, little more for the fish curry and the rest of the rice that he wanted to be the largest for the mutton curry. He proceeded accordingly.

A problem occurred after he finished with the rice quota for the dal and brinjal fries. He found the fish curry so tasty that he failed to adhere to the fixed quota and made heavy inroads into the largest quota left for the mutton curry. And then Bhogmon started praying in his mind.

'Please, please, sis! Go into the kitchen and pray bring the rice bowl back, filled to the rim!' he began repeating the prayers as the he fiddled with the remaining rice and the mutton pieces as a time-pass strategy, trying to send a signal to Renu that it was rice that he so badly needed. But all three of them were busy with their plates, occasionally engaging themselves in a casual banter. But were they eating at all, he wondered? They were not eating; they were only pecking on their plates! 'Maybe normal devour is eating and dieting is pecking!' he wondered still.

It was just not about the quantity of rice which was not sufficient for his curries! It was more about him having to leave the dining table with his stomach half empty! He detested the idea of recompensing the rice with more of the salad. Anyway, salad is never one of his favourites! He knows that there are so many items recommended for good health and hygiene; but as a true discerning connoisseur of good food, he cannot afford to follow that completely!

He repeated his prayers once again, more in the way of Mayday! But to no avail!

So, he finished his meal along with the others. At the earliest opportunity while back at the living room he excused himself saying that an old friend was expected back home early afternoon. They didn't mind that too much, because in the fitness book of Renu a brief afternoon nap which is often called a power nap is always most welcome. Bhogmon somehow forced a smile as he said goodbye to them and came out, and readying his bicycle he rang the bell briefly, winking at Maina. And then he cycled away home.

He parked the cycle quietly in the front courtyard and entered his mother's room stealthily. She was lying on her bed with a book. He accosted her and explained the matter in detail. Concern overshadowed her endearing face even as she couldn't quite hide a smile.

"Okay, dear! Don't you worry! I'll do the needful! But don't make noise, Charu is sleeping! Of course, the kids haven't returned and Rong is out at the Panchayat meeting." She put the book away and slowly got up from the bed heading for the kitchen area. On the way she turned and asked smiling, "Are you hungry already?"

"Not exactly at the moment! But I'll be in about ten minutes!"

"No problem! But don't discuss these things with anyone, right? You see, such gossip finally harms the atmosphere." She said as she moved away.

Bhogmon went to his room and changed into a short and a vest. Moments later he joined his mother in the kitchen.

His mother had already put the rice in the big saucepan for boil. She used the traditional way of cooking rice that allowed her to strain the starch from it whenever she was at her original home. As Bhogmon sat in the middle compartment of the kitchen that had a clay floor where they still used to sit upon while being served meals on the brass plates, he remembered the old times some of which he managed to get first hand, at a tender age though.

On many occasions one or two of his father's farm labourers were called to their house to help in domestic matters. On all such occasions his mother invariably served them lunch. What lunches those were, he cherished the memories: huge pyramids of rice set upon either banana leaves or on the large brass plates; on the peak of the pyramid some dal was sprinkled in and along with it just the indication of a vegetable item; on the sides there were pieces of the country lemon, a few green chillies and pinches of salt, at times the salt was immersed with a few drops of mustard oil.

There was simply not enough curry or dal or *bhaji* to take the rice with, he went on reliving the memories, but how happily they ate! It was the rice that mattered to most of the villagers. They could take the rice with just a pinch of salt and green chillies if that was what was required. How they enjoyed having it still! Images of that *thali* prepared by his mother for them kept on coming to his mind over the years and every time the images made his mouth water. Yes! It's the rice that matters to him too! All other items are only complementing, not overtaking! It's another matter that he enjoys the rich varieties of dishes, preparations and items greatly, but always with rice, and rice only!

And now he's ravenously hungry as his mother spreads the steaming rice across the traditional brass plate placed on the floor before him. His mother informs that not much's been left of the dal or the curries. How does it matter? He has the rice! Bhogmon starts eating!

***

About the Author

Chinmay Chakravarty

Award winning author Chinmay Chakravarty is a professional specialized in the creative field with over three decades of experience in journalistic writing, media co-ordination, film script writing, film dubbing, film & video making and management of international film festivals. He has been writing articles, news stories, short fiction and short stories since his student days and throughout his long service career in the media sector of the Government of India. Chinmay has published his first book 'Laugh and Let Laugh' in 2017 and the book got a nomination for India Authors Award-2021 organized by NMCBI in Mumbai. His second book in pure fiction, 'The Cheerless Chauffeur and Other Tales', published in 2021, earned him an award as the 'Emerging Author of the Year—Fiction' in Literary Awards-2022, organized by Ukiyoto Publishing in

Kolkata. His books published by Ukiyoto Publishing are 'The Astral Limbo' (2022) and 'The Weirdos' (2022-23). He also has several titles on Amazon KDP.

www.ingramcontent.com/pod-product-compliance
Lightning Source LLC
LaVergne TN
LVHW041222080526
838199LV00082B/2082